Saint George
and the Dragon

Written by
GERALDINE McCAUGHREAN

Illustrated by
NICKI PALIN

OXFORD
UNIVERSITY PRESS

THE still, deep pool lay in a hollow below the high wooden fence of the hilltop town. Every day the women came down to draw its water. Their sheep drank at its banks, and a few straggling roses bloomed, in coils of bramble, along the water's edge.

Then, one morning, the women walking down to the water dropped their empty buckets, ran back, and closed the city gates, sobbing with fright. Climbing to the top of the pallisade, they peeped over.

A dragon, born in the deepest crevices of the bottomless pool, had dragged itself out on to the bank and lay coiled around it.

A wreath of sinew and claw. Its red mouth gaped as it panted in the hot sun. Its ragged teeth bulged through rolled green lips. And awake or asleep, its lidless eyes stared and its claws stretched and withdrew, stretched and withdrew in the waterside mud. Its foul breath hung in a green haze. Its father was Evil, its mother Darkness, and its name was Wickedness.

That night it left the pool, lifting its heavy haunches and heaving its scaled belly off the ground. Lizard-like, it cut a track through the mud, dragging its thorny tail. The people herded their livestock into the city and shut the gates on the dragon.

But what good is a wooden fence against breath fuming with fire? One corner of the town was set ablaze, and its crumbling ash blew away in the morning wind.

The dragon ate two dogs, before thrashing back to the pool to coil itself around the water.

Next day, the people opened the gates just wide enough to push two sheep out on to the plain. The animals stood bleating, then trotted down towards the water in the hollow. Suddenly, the shape of the dragon lurched up over them! Fleece and flesh, it tore them to pieces.

Two sheep were fed to the dragon every day, though sometimes, after its meal, it would still slither towards the city and scratch its back against the timber fence.

From the high window of the palace, Princess Sabra watched with a pale face, and asked: 'What will happen when there are no more sheep?'

Before the last sheep was gone, the people began to draw lots in the most terrible of lotteries. The name of every man, woman and child was entered, and one name drawn out each day: one person to be turned out of the city, side by side with a sheep as food for the dragon.

Soon, the sound of wailing hung like a cloud over the city. Men eyed one another across the street and thought: 'I hope his name will be drawn before mine.'

One day, the wailing came from the palace itself. The Princess Sabra's name had been drawn in the lottery.

'No! I forbid it!' cried the King.

'It is the law,' said the town governors. 'You made it so.'

'But she is so good and pure, and I love her so very much!'

'We loved our daughters,' said the old women, 'but still they were fed to the dragon when their turn came.'

'But she's so small and fragile—a poor morsel for a hungry dragon!'

'Then go in her place!' shouted the people. 'What good have you been to us since the dragon came?'

And when he saw rebellion in their faces, the King gave up his daughter. 'Don't let me see her again, or I may change my mind.'

Not far away, a horseman was riding
up a steep hill when his horse stopped and
began to paw the ground, blowing sharply through
its nostrils. The rider himself was aware of a charred,
acrid smell in the air. From the top of the hill,
he looked down on devastation.

In the hollow below, there lay a fouled and festering pool. Beyond it, a fortified town had its gates closed in siege.

Turning its head idly in his direction, a dragon, its flightless wings half spread, paused in its slinking, lizard-like scuttle, and let out a roar.

The flash of sunlight on a bridle, and the white of the horse itself, had caught the dragon's eye. At the same moment, a speck of white and gold flickered to its left: a golden-haired maiden dressed in a lightly blowing smock was being tied to the stake where the beast looked daily for its dinner.

The girl cast one imploring look towards the town. But the windows of her father's palace were empty. Her head fell forward in despair.

The dragon threw out a contemptuous roar at the rider and turned to devour its white morsel of meat. . . .

'Hear this, beast, that I am George of Lydda, and a pure man!'
The rider's voice barely reached the dragon across the wilderness.
'Turn and fight me—for surely your father was Evil, your mother
Darkness, and you are Wickedness itself!' George levelled his long
lance.

The dragon's jaws—gaping over the Princess—clashed shut.
It snaked on its haunches, and its wings beat the air.

A column of fuming fire belched from its nostrils.
But the soldier, galloping towards it across the plain,
raised a shield over his own and his horse's head,
and the fire was turned aside. The brightness
of the sun on shield and helmet seemed to
madden the rampaging beast.

George's noble white horse carried him into the very shadow of the dragon. Its green paw reached out to snatch him from his saddle. The lance slapped the dragon's shoulder, but the scales were tough like leather, rough like stone.

Horse and dragon cannoned together. The mare's foamy sweat spattered the dragon's green flank. A moment later, the massive tail lashed round, but the horse stood back on its haunches and sprang across its thorns.

George's lance struck the beast's snout and shattered like an icicle.

For a moment, he stared into the lidless eyes, then he threw up his shield again, to keep off the cauldron-breath.

The dragon struck him a blow with its horny wing that pitched him to the ground. George threw off his helmet, and snatched the broad sword from his saddle.

As vast jaws opened to devour the soldier where he stood, he ran in under the towering green chest and plunged in the sword where a heart should lie.

But the creature had no heart!

A spurt of black blood spattered George's shield. But the dragon only threw back its head and gave a gargled roar. Its claws tore the young man's cloak into seven ragged strips.

Once more George drove in the sword—drove it into the gaping red jaw. It was torn from his grasp as the beast thrashed its head from side to side.

For a moment, the lumbering body threatened to capsize and crush George. And as he put both hands on the dragon's flank to push it away, smoke rose from the palms of his gloves. With the groaning slowness of a falling tree, the creature crashed down on to its side.

George left it where it lay, and ran to the side
of the Princess, lifted up her face, and said:
'The danger is almost past. I see that you are
a pure and lovely maiden. Give me your sash,
please, for the dragon is not dead.'
        With the sash, he circled the lolling
green head.

In the depths of the beast's cavernous body, its furious fire was extinguished. In the depths of its eyes, too, the wildness and wickedness went out. The vanquished dragon laid down its head on George's lap: its breathing calm, its breath harmless to the sweet and unscorched air.

Together, Sabra and George led a peaceful dragon through the streets of the town and it lay down at the gates of the palace.

'Stranger,' said the delighted King, 'where you are from I do not know. But end your journey here, with my palace for your home and my daughter for your wife!'

'I cannot,' said George, (though he looked at the Princess with longing in his eyes). 'I have other dragons to vanquish.'

His horse was brought to him, her white mane scorched and her white tail charred. And slipping his arm from between Sabra's two white hands, George mounted and rode away.

Though Sabra watched for him from the window of the highest palace tower, he never returned.

Some people say that he took ship and travelled to other countries and fought other dragons.

Even after a thousand years, some said they had seen him, still wielding his sword and blood-splashed shield, still fighting dragony Death.

But no memory survives of the place where George finally lay down his sword and slept.

Some say his grave lies in Persia in a place where blood-red roses flourish their blossoms through toils of briar, beside still, deep water.

English soldiers, returning from a brutal
and bloody war, swore they had seen George—
his white banner crossed with blood—and
that his encouragement had saved them.
In gratitude, they blazoned the memory
of him on their armour and their flags,
and called him England's own
Saint George.

AFTERWORD

The details of the life of George the Saint are few and uncertain. Even the execution exacted by Emperor Diocletian on 23 April AD 303 may have been another man, another among the numberless Christian martyrs. But that he lived and died is proven: it is his death which is commemorated on Saint George's Day.

The exploits of George the Dragon-slayer are altogether more vivid—adventures of a sort that were being told with relish 2,000 years ago. English Crusaders carried home the stories, adding a story of their own—of a vision that rallied them at the battle of Antioch in 1309. They acted out his fight in their Miracle plays, vaunted him in their church windows, took him so to heart that Edward III lighted on him in 1348 as a fit patron for England.

And yet the Dragon-slayer was an amalgamation of shadows, a pooling of myths. He is the Greek Perseus who saved Andromeda from the sea monster; Christ who slays the satanic beast in *Revelation*; Renewal which conquers Death; Good which conquers Evil. The Slayer probably never existed: he is a figment of universal imagination. But he stepped out of folklore to the aid of an obscure young man ingloriously tortured to death long ago in Asia Minor. As a result the young man was immortalized: Saint George, Patron Saint of England.

OXFORD
UNIVERSITY PRESS

Great Clarendon Street, Oxford OX2 6DP

Oxford is the trade mark of Oxford University Press

Text © Geraldine McCaughrean 1989
Illustrations © Nicki Palin 1989
First published in 1989
First published in paperback 1994
Reissued in this paperback edition 2000

British Library Cataloguing in Publication Data
McCaughrean, Geraldine
Saint George and the Dragon.
I. Title 823'.914[F] PZ7
ISBN : 978-0-19-272376-5

12 14 16 18 20 19 17 15 13

Printed in Hong Kong

Paper used in the production of this book is a natural, recyclable product
made from wood grown in sustainable forests. The manufacturing process
conforms to the environmental regulations of the country of origin.